This book belongs to

....

Written by Sarah Phillips.
Illustrated by Stuart Lynch.

Pennie the pinkest polar bear

Sarah Phillips · Stuart Lynch

make
believe
ideas

Pennie's a friendly polar bear,
but she is very, very shy.
She stammers as she says her name
and often starts to cry.

She blushes pink from head to toe
and can't think of what to say.
Who wants to play with a PINK bear?
So she usually runs away.

"You need to keep your **throat** warm with something **woolly** and **thick!**" says **Dan.** "My bark is **always** clear. This **scarf** will do the **trick.**"

"Now let's **stretch** and **twist** our necks and try some **short**, sharp **sounds**."

So they **cough** and **bark** and stand up **tall** and **wind** their **heads** around.

Later on a cool new cat comes sauntering down the street. Pennie runs up to say hello, but stammers and retreats.

Cool Cat's shocked
but understands.
She knows just what to do.

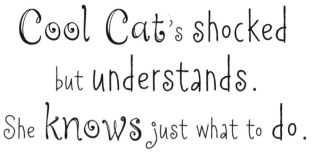

"Come and drink
my special milk.
It'll soothe your
throat for you."

Pennie and Cool Cat sip the milk,
warmed and mixed with honey.
They even try some "singing,"
but Dan doesn't find that funny!

As Pennie runs back through the park,
she meets the Treetop Twins.

"H-h-hi, I-I'M P-P-P-...!" she stammers,
before escaping to the swings.

The Treetop Twins
know how to help.
They say, "We have no doubt,
if you learn to say our
tongue-twisters
it will sort the
stammering out!"

Just then the traveling pigs arrive
with big bags and a ball.
"H-hi, I'm P-P-P-....!" Pennie cries,
before her tears begin to fall.

"Come with us," the kind pigs say,
"Let's **all** have some **fun**.

We'll **dance** and **sing** together,
and **join** the others **Later on!**"

"Pink is the perfect color!

That's what **we** both say.

Enjoy the fact that you turn pink

and hope to stay that way!"

As the moon shines in the sky and stars start to twinkle,

the hushed friends inside the tent
hear **silver bells** that tinkle...

In comes Pennie, dressed in pink. She does a dance, and sings, "I'm Pennie the pinkest polar bear, and I want to say these things:

You're very welcome to the show. We hope you enjoy it all. There's dancing, music, acrobatics, and a very special ball!"

Pennie sits down, pink as pink,
and smiles at all her friends.
She's wowed by the amazing acts
and loves the mice at the end.

Pennie is walking home with Dan;
they're dancing as they go.

"Pink is the perfect color — I want everyone to know!"

Don't be **upset** at how you are.
Enjoy yourself and **see**
that the **more** you gain in **confidence**,
the **happier** you'll be!